LOOK AND FIND®

Written by Melanie Zanoza
Based on the original screenplay by Chris McKenna
Illustrated by Art Mawhinney

Published by Louis Weber, C.E.O.
Publications International, Ltd.
7373 North Cicero Avenue, Lincolnwood, Illinois 60712
Ground Floor, 59 Gloucester Place, London WIU 8JJ

Customer Service: 1-800-595-8484
or customer_service@pilbooks.com

www.pilbooks.com

Manufactured in China.

8 7 6 5 4 3 2 1

ISBN-13: 978-1-4127-9401-5
ISBN-10: 1-4127-9401-3

Welcome to Malaria, where evil scientists compete each year to produce the world's most devastating invention. But one doctor's assistant is ready to do a little creating of his own. Look for Igor, then find these other busy assistants.

Dr. Schadenfreude, winner of the past 17 Evil Science Fairs, is holding his annual pre-fair party. Find him, then look around the partygoers for these mad scientist guests.

Dr. Schadenfreude

Dr. Herzschlag

Dr. Holzwurm

Dr. Kindermann

Dr. Niemand

Dr. Blitzkrieg

With his scientist suddenly gone, Igor can finally work on his newest and most important creation in peace. As he adds the Evil Bone and prepares to flip the switch, look for these parts and pieces the new scientist chose not to use.

Adam's apple

Spare ribs

Wish bone

Hare brain

Funny bone

Sugar & spice

Frogs, snails, puppy-dogs' tails

Igor's creation is alive...and on the loose in an orphanage. As Igor thinks of a way to get her home, look for these children who are thrilled with their new playmate.

Midnight Mae Hemm

Banshee Tombstone

Damien Dervish

Dementia Forgetmenot

Boo Johnson

Arachna Fo-Bia

Dirge O'Deathknell

Igor has brought Eva to the brainwash in hopes of activating her Evil Bone. As she receives her wash, look for these other treatment options.

Scary Clown

Zombie

Vampire

Rabid Monkey

Werewolf

Piranha Frenzy

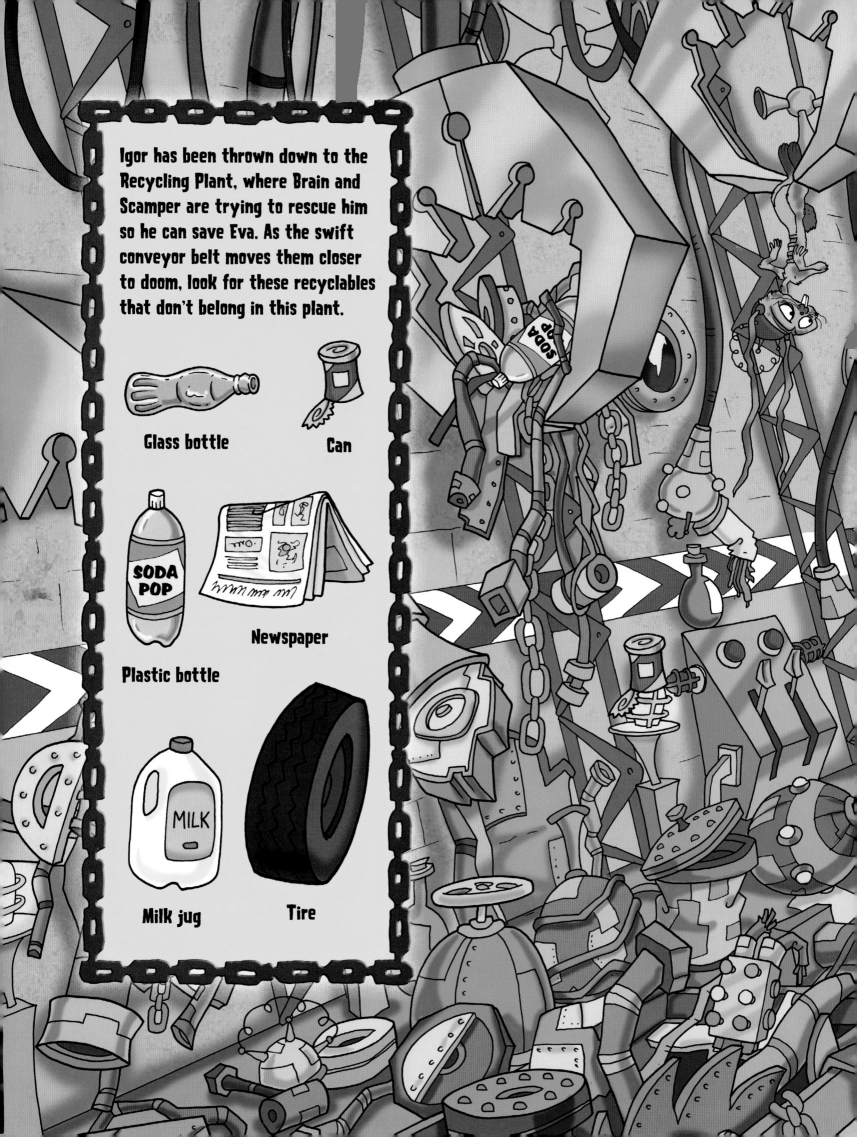

Igor has been thrown down to the Recycling Plant, where Brain and Scamper are trying to rescue him so he can save Eva. As the swift conveyor belt moves them closer to doom, look for these recyclables that don't belong in this plant.

Glass bottle

Can

Plastic bottle

SODA POP

Newspaper

Milk jug

MILK

Tire

At the Killiseum, Eva's Evil Bone has finally been activated, and she's ready for a fight. As she battles the rest of the Evil Science Fair inventions, look around the stadium for these extreme fans.

Igor and friends are back at the Killiseum...which has become the Malaria Community Theater! As Eva prepares her cast for their performance, look for these props and costumes she has chosen not to use.

Glasses

Top hat

Ballet shoes and tutu

Cane

Cowboy hat

Parasol

Glittery shoes

Others besides Igors are at work in Malaria, too. Can you spot them?

Garbage collector

Chimney sweep

Street cleaner

Mail carrier

Baker

Nanny

Boogie back to the party and look for these evil delicacies the doctor served.

Punch

Finger sandwiches

Deviled eggs

Jalapeño poppers

Monster hash

Brain freeze

Kung-pow! chicken

Dr. Glickenstein kept many useful tools and ingredients. Zap yourself back to his lab and look for these supplies.

ANGER SERUM

Anger serum

False teeth

Eye of newt

Shrink gun

INSTANT PERSONALITY POWDER

Instant personality powder

Duct tape

Eva is enchanted by the paper flowers the orphans make. Twirl back to the Home for Blind Orphans and look for 21 pink flowers.

Slosh your way back to the brainwash and look for these greeting cards Scamper has been perusing.

HAPPY EVIL SCIENCE FAIR DAY!

HAPPY FATHER'S DAY!

UNHAPPY BIRTHDAY!

WISHING YOU BAD LUCK!

WISH YOU WERE'NT THERE!

HAPPY MOTHER'S DAY

Return to the Recycling Plant and look for these gears, tools, and parts.

Battle your way back to the Killiseum to look for Eva and some of the Evil Inventions she faced.

Venus flytrap

Eva

Teddy bear

Orb

Blob monster

Animal robot

Head back to the Malaria Community Theater and see if you can spot the concessions She-gor Heidi and Dr. Schadenfreude will be selling.

Cotton candy

Pickles

Hot cocoa

Hot dog

STRUDEL

Strudel

Popcorn